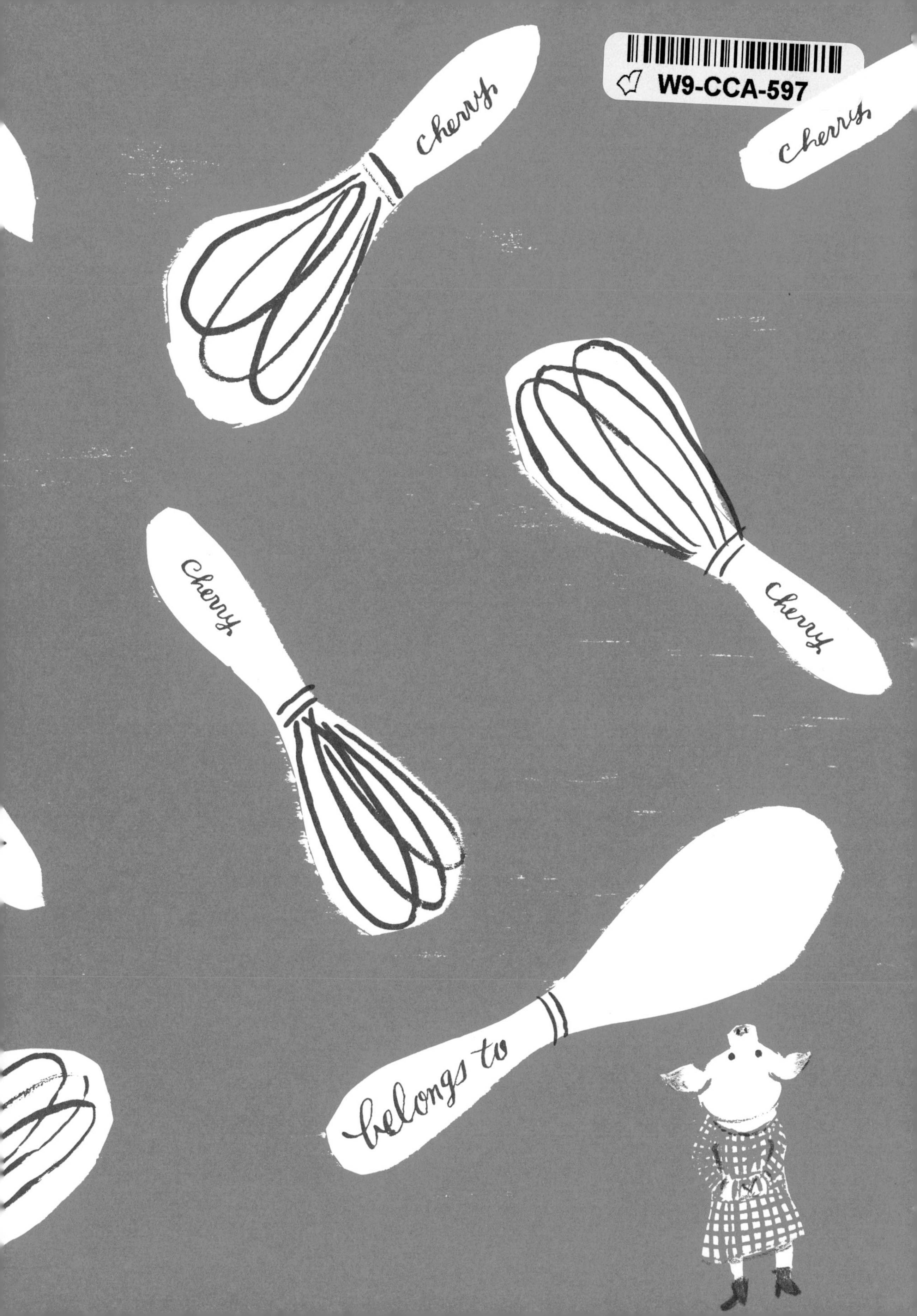
cherry
cherry
cherry
cherry
belongs to

To Haruka

THE STORY OF

Cherry the Pig

Utako Yamada

Cherry the pig lived in a pretty little village known for its delicate willow trees and sweet, home-grown fruit.

Now all pigs love to eat, and Cherry was no exception. What she especially loved to eat though, was dessert. During lunch, she would look through her recipes. Then, as soon as lunch was over, she would make an enormous dessert and eat the whole thing herself. (She was, after all, a pig.)

One day, she decided to make an apple cake.

Apple Cake
My Recipes

When Cherry took the cake out of the oven it was a magnificent golden color. Its sweet cinnamon smell filled the room, and made her mouth water.

Cherry put the cake on the table to cool and turned her back to make tea. Then, all of sudden, she heard…

"It's incredible!"

"Oh, it is!"

wake up!
wake up!
Sweet home
Cinnamon
Raisins
Sugar
Good tea

Cherry looked over to see a family of mice enjoying her cake.
"Stop!" she yelled, and the mouse family scattered.

Cherry poured herself a cup of milky tea, cut away the parts of the cake that had been nibbled, and picked up her fork.

The apples were sweet; the cake was light and fluffy. The mice were right – it was incredible! An apple cake this good should be shared. Cherry decided to enter her incredible apple cake in the bake-off at the Harvest Festival.

She went right out and signed up.

On the day of the Harvest Festival, booths and stands lined the village square.

Ring! Ring!

The lemonade stand bell signaled the start of the bake-off. Cherry was ready!

Snap apple . game
ear lover
Lemonade
Lemonade

She gathered her ingredients, whipped the butter and the sugar, cracked the eggs,

and beat them into the mix.

She chopped apples, adding them to the bowl with the spices and the flour.

She worked skillfully, moving quickly and with care.

Then, all of a sudden…

“Do you see who that is?! It’s the pig!” Cherry heard the mice laugh. “Why in the world would she enter that incredibly awful cake in the bake-off?”

Cherry was stunned. Is that what the mice had said in her kitchen? Incredibly *awful*?

Tears rolled down her face.

Cherry put her cake in the oven. Then, sad and disheartened, she went to sit by herself in the shade of a tree.

Soon the air around her was filled with sweet, sugary smells, and an announcement came over the loudspeaker.

"Please proceed to the main stage. The winners of the bake-off will be announced in five minutes."

Slowly, Cherry got up. She didn't really want to go, but she did.

The village mayor was standing on the stage holding three whisks – one gold, one silver, and one bronze.

"Now, without further ado, I am pleased to announce that the winner of third place in the bake-off and the bronze whisk is... Jane the cow! Her mouthwatering caramels are so good you'll want them to last forever.

Second place and the silver whisk go to...Mamie the chicken! Her mint tart will wake up your mouth and open your eyes – it's perfect for breakfast!

And the grand prize winner of this year's bake-off and the recipient of the gold whisk is…
Cherry the pig! Her apple cake is so delicious one slice just isn't enough!"

Was it true? Was she hearing right? Cherry couldn't believe it. How did her incredibly awful cake win first prize?

After the awards ceremony, the bake-off entries were served. Everyone loved Cherry's cake.
"This is the best apple cake I've ever tasted."
"It's so light and fluffy."
"I need another piece!"
As Cherry thanked her friends for their kind words, she thought about the mice. Why did they say her cake was so awful?

She looked around for the mice, but she couldn't find them. What she did find was the tiny, mouse-sized bag of biscuits they'd left behind. She broke off a piece of one the biscuits to taste. It was very hard, very salty, very cheesy, and…incredibly awful. "Oh," thought Cherry. "So this is what they like."

Returning home, Cherry thought about everything that had happened. It was all because she had misunderstood the mice. She thought too, of her neighbors' faces, and how they had looked as they were eating her cake. And then she thought about how happy it had made her feel to bake something that others enjoyed.

Cherry decided to start a bakery.

On opening day, the villagers crowded the bakery, smiling and laughing and buying almost everything.

apple B

It was a very busy day.

But Cherry still had one more thing to make.

A present for the mice. Very hard, very salty, very cheesy biscuits.

Dear mice,

How about these? Aren't they incredible?

Cherry

Kane/Miller Book Publishers, Inc.
First American Edition 2007
by Kane/Miller Book Publishers, Inc.
La Jolla, California

Originally published in Japan by Kaisei-Sha Publishers, Inc.

Kane/Miller Book Publishers, Inc.
P.O. Box 8515
La Jolla, CA 92038
www.kanemiller.com

Library of Congress Control Number: 2006931564
Printed and bound in China
2 3 4 5 6 7 8 9 10

ISBN: 978-1-933605-25-8

cherry